THE SHROUD OF TURIN
AND THE C-14 DATING FIASCO:

A SCIENTIFIC DETECTIVE STORY

D1070091

THE SHROUD OF TURIN
AND THE C-14 DATING FIASCO:

A SCIENTIFIC DETECTIVE STORY

Thomas W. Case

White Horse Press
Cincinnati

First Edition 1996

Third Printing, March 1997

©1996 Thomas W. Case
All Rights Reserved

Cover photo and all photographs in this book
provided by Vernon Miller Associates
©Vernon D. Miller, 1978

ISBN 0-9648310-1-5

Library of Congress
Catalog Card Number 96-60013

White Horse Press
6723 Betts Ave.
Cincinnati, Ohio 45239

Printed by Northern Printing
Cincinnati, OH 45246

Dedicated to the memory of John H. Heller,
whose curiosity was aroused by the phrase
"physics of miracles" in a 1978 *Science* article;
whose exacting chemical analysis proved that
the Shroud image could not be a forgery;
and who passed into the hands of God
on December 13, 1995.

Requiescat in pace

CONTENTS

The positive film image on the left shows a flat, blotchy portrait. The actual image on the Shroud is straw yellow, more diffuse looking, and even disappears when viewed close up. The film negative on the right shows a vivid 3-D portrait. It is as if the Shroud image itself were a negative print, making the "negative of the negative" an actual view of the Man on the Shroud.

 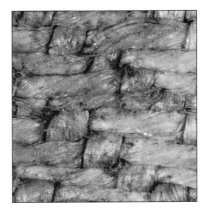

A VP-8 computerized rendition of a photo of the head on the Shroud. Such an undistorted 3-D effect is ordinarily impossible to attain from a two dimensional picture.

A microphotograph of the weave, showing blood stains. That these stains really *are* blood was determined by means of exacting chemical tests performed by Drs. Heller and Adler.

FOREWORD

On December 13, 1995 Doctor John Heller departed this life after spending a lifetime of study, teaching, research, experiment and accomplishment in the field of chemistry. With Dr. Alan Adler, Dr. Heller devoted a significant portion of his life and career to the study of the Holy Shroud of Turin. While the emphasis of the team of "Heller and Adler" was on the science of chemistry as it pertained to the Holy Shroud, they both gave witness to the more sensitive meaning and truth behind the mystery of the Shroud of Turin. Their collaboration with the "Shroud of Turin Research Project" (STURP) produced the now classic article, "A Chemical Investigation of the Shroud of Turin." They popularized among the religious community the scientific concepts behind words like "microchemical testing, textiles, the iron-oxide of blood, protein, linen fibrils, cellulose and pigments." John Heller was one of the great giants among the multi-disciplinary procession of scientists who committed the resources and observations of their technology to this ancient Christian relic. He was always a professional, and combined in a unique way the science of chemistry with the faith of a disciple. He was truly a renaissance man who combined the resources of science with great measures of his devotion. I will miss Doctor John Heller and the unique contribution he made to Holy Shroud research during the second half of the 20th Century.

Science and religion writer Thomas Case has put together a vivid account which summarizes and condenses the thousands of hours of work which the team of Heller and Adler put into its research of the Shroud of Turin. With insightful commentary and transcripts of conversations with Heller and Adler, Mr. Case draws his own conclusions and makes his own contributions to the study of the Holy Shroud. This present volume will be a necessary addition to the libraries of those who support the scientific investigation of the Holy Shroud of Turin.

Rev. Frederick C. Brinkmann, C.Ss.R.
President pro tem
Holy Shroud Guild
Esopus, New York

INTRODUCTION

This book contains a lengthy personal interview with Shroud of Turin scientists John H. Heller and Alan D. Adler. The author talked with them for over five hours in Dr. Heller's home on July 18, 1994. The two biochemists, not members of the original 1978 STURP team who travelled to Italy to examine the Shroud, are nevertheless the most important of the many Shroud experts. It is their painstaking chemical analysis, carried on over a period of several years, that established once and for all that the Shroud Image could not have been a forgery.

They proved that the blood on the Shroud is real blood. They proved that the Image is the result of an acid-like oxidation of the top-most crowns of individual fibers on the linen burial cloth. This is what produced the straw-yellow color of the Image. The Image could not have been the result of painting or human artistry of any kind.

The two chemists also offer a considered criticism of the Radiocarbon tests performed in 1988 and which purport to date the Shroud at around 1300 A.D.

An accompanying essay gives a background for the science presented in the interview, describes the very strange optics of the Shroud, and reveals the recent experiments performed by two Russian scientists, Drs. Dmitri Kouznetsov and Andrey Ivanov. These new experiments demonstrate the effects of the 1532 fire on Carbon-14 time-testing. Without giving away too much of the story in this short preview, it can be said that a combination of reactions involving carbon-exchange could very easily have thrown off the 1988 Radiocarbon test date by some 1300 years.

PART I

THE PHYSICS OF A MIRACLE

In 1978 the Shroud of Turin Research Project—a group of some forty American scientists—were allowed to travel to Italy to examine the famous relic. They performed a multitude of non-destructive tests, from photography to microscopy and spectrographic analysis. They took samples of the Shroud's topmost fibers by means of small strips of Mylar tape pressed lightly against various portions of the cloth. It was the most extensive scientific examination the Shroud had ever undergone.

Back in the States, the STURP team sent a number of these fibril-encrusted tapes to Dr. Walter McCrone. McCrone had a certain reputation as an expert in microscopic analysis, and had gained renown as the man who had exposed a supposed Viking map of the New World (owned by Yale University) as a modern forgery. (But now there is some question about his negative judgment on that map.) Now McCrone published a report—in his own magazine, *Microscope*—that claimed the Shroud of Turin was a medieval fake. He had found particles of iron oxide and cinnabar. He theorized that an artist had made red ochre paint from iron oxide and mixed it into a gelatin base, and then applied it to the cloth to paint the image. He decided that the cinnabar, which is bright red in color and contains mercuric sulphide, went into a mixture, again with iron oxide, to make the "blood" which appears here and there on the cloth. He claimed that medieval artists had used both cinnabar and iron oxide to make red and rust colored paints.

There were, however, many reasons to think the Shroud was not a forgery, but the genuine burial cloth of a crucified man—and that McCrone was dead wrong in his analysis. Chemical experiments performed by John Heller and Alan Adler demonstrated that the blood was real blood. The two scientists discovered serum and blood clots, blood proteins, hemoglobins, and blood break-down products like bilirubin. They determined that the Image was made not by paint, but by oxidation and dehydration of the top-most fibrils on the cloth. The straw yellow (not rusty) color of the Image arrived by an oxidation process similar to the yellowing of table linen with age.

Meanwhile x-ray analysis as well had shown no significant evidence of elements on the Image that could have come from paint. Specifically, cinnabar was ruled out as a constituent of the "blood," and iron oxide was ruled out as a constituent of the Image. Further chemical analysis ruled out any possible artists' pigments of whatever color. Ultraviolet analysis showed that the Image did not fluoresce. Since scorched linen fluoresces, the Image could not be a scorch (as from the application of heat), though that is what it resembles.

Most riveting was the work done by Eric Jumper and John Jackson, who used a VP-8 Analyzer—a computerized tool used to enhance the qualities of photographs taken by space probes—to arrive at a perfectly exact three dimensional rendition of the negative of the Image. It was as if we had, on the cloth, a perfect mirror image of the man it had once covered. The reverse of that cloth image—its "photographic negative"—reveals the original subject of the "photograph" in vivid 3-D detail.

McCrone stood alone in his judgment of fakery. Adler, Heller, Eric Jumper, John Jackson, Ray Rogers and the other STURP and non-STURP scientists had gone into the project expecting to find some artistic procedure that could have made the Image. They could not. They could prove to an overwhelming degree of probability that the Shroud was not a forgery, but they also could not find any chemical or physical or biological process—in any combination—to account for the properties of the Image.

Ideology soon entered the scenario. A small group of skeptical journalists and scientists came up with theory after theory trying to debunk the Shroud's authenticity. On the other hand, many of the STURP scientists who had started out skeptical were converted to religious belief *by means of the experimental science they had performed.* The STURP scientists as a whole then became branded as a covey of religious fanatics—despite the fact that they had the most rigorous, and rigorously peer reviewed, science on their side.

This is important to understand. There was no religious bias to begin with. Although some of the STURP team adhered to various religious beliefs, they were as one in approaching their subject in a purely scientific manner: to verify what they could verify by means of exacting experiments. What happened is that experiment after experiment and test after test ruled out any and all natural explanations. The scientists were left with an enigma. Some of them were brave enough to realize that science in this case had led beyond science. Science itself had opened onto the supernatural.

Everyone involved in scientific Shroud study begged the Vatican to allow radiocarbon dating. This would finally confirm the age of the relic, if not the manner of its making.

In 1988 radiocarbon dating was finally performed. So as to keep damage to a minimum, the sample was cut from a corner of the Shroud near the place where another sample had been taken in 1973. It was cut into three parts and sent to three different laboratories, in Oxford, in Arizona, and in Zurich. Eventually the bad news came in. C14 dating declared the Shroud to be medieval, the linen (it was said) having been made somewhere between 1260 and 1390 A.D. The Shroud was, after all, a forgery. So it seemed.

Popular and scientific journals gleefully reported the "fraud." In its November 1988 issue, *Scientific American* interviewed Walter McCrone—to the exclusion of anyone else. McCrone repeated his hypothesis: the "blood" was vermillion paint (mercuric sulphide) and the image was made by red ochre (a paint made from iron oxide) which was mixed into a gelatin base. *Scientific American* published a color photo in the lower left hand corner of the page, yellowish and showing globs of orange somethings, labeled "Particles of Red Ochre in a gelatin-based medium tint the surface of the Shroud of Turin. The micrograph is by Walter C. McCrone."

Well, you can see it in a picture, so it must be true. And if *Scientific American* says it's particles of red ochre, it must be particles of red ochre.

End of story? Not so fast. McCrone's hypothesis, having been promoted by him for the previous ten years, had found no corroboration by chemists, physicists, computer analysts, forensic experts, archaeologists, or any others who in their various fields of expertise had studied the Shroud over that same decade from 1978 to 1988.

THE BLOOD ON THE SHROUD

Scientists who want to publish in top-flight scientific journals (I do not mean *Scientific American*) must submit their research papers to an exacting process called "peer review." The editors must be satisfied that the science is legitimate. This is why such papers are usually first published in journals whose editorial review board is fully conversant with the subject at hand. Other scientists with expertise in the field under consideration are invited to subject the experiments, the statistical analysis, the graphs and charts, the reasoning and the conclusions, to exacting criticism. Heller's and Adler's chemical and biophysical reports went through such a rigorous peer review. McCrone's didn't. McCrone published in his own journal, *Microscope,* without any peer review at all.

Heller and Adler published their findings in an article titled "A Chemical Investigation of the Shroud of Turin," in the *Canadian Society for Forensic Science Journal,* Vol.14, No.3 (1981). For our purposes it is important to take note of the exhaustive studies the two chemists performed to answer the question of whether or not the "blood" on the Shroud was real blood. They summarized their results in a list duplicated below. The language is technical, but as you look over the list, note that "Fe" is iron, a constituent of blood. Note that "heme" is the chemical word for the iron-containing pigment in the hemoglobin molecule in blood. Note also that albumin is a protein found in blood. Finally you should know that bile pigments are found especially in blood that has been broken down, after severe trauma, and passed through the liver. Bile is the stuff that produces the yellow color of jaundice. Now take a close look at the results of the tests performed by Heller and Adler:

1. High Fe in blood areas by X-ray fluorescence
2. Indicative reflection spectra
3. Indicative microspectrophotometric transmission spectra
4. Chemical generation of characteristic porphyrin fluorescence
5. Positive hemochromogen tests
6. Positive cyanmethemoglobin tests
7. Positive detection of bile pigments
8. Positive demonstration of protein
9. Positive indication of albumin specifically
10. Protease tests, leaving no residues
11. Microscopic appearance as compared with appropriate controls
12. Forensic judgment of the appearance of the various wounds and blood marks

Heller, in his 1983 book *Report on the Shroud of Turin*, takes note that any one of these: the reflection scan, the microspectrophotometric scan, the positive hemochromogen test, the positive bile test, the positive cyanomethemoglobin test, the heme porphyrin fluorescence—is forensic proof in a court of law that blood is present. Taken together, the proof is irrefutable.

The forensic evidence demonstrates the presence of about 120 scourge marks (some visible only under ultraviolet light), primarily on the back and shoulders of the figure. There is a mass of blood dripping from the crown of the head, from the puncture wounds in the hands and feet, and from a wound in the side. All the forensic evidence conforms in detail to the Gospel renditions of the Crucifixion of Jesus Christ.

Reputable scientific conclusion #1:

THE BLOOD ON THE SHROUD IS REAL BLOOD.

THE IMAGE

The Image has been determined by the same two chemists—Heller and Adler—to be the result of chemical degradation of the crowns of the top-most fibrils in the Image area. This degradation fits most closely the operation of acid on linen. It first of all involves dehydration: a severe drying out process. Secondly it is oxidation, the mild forms of which produce a yellowing or browning, the more severe forms of which produce a scorch, a char, and finally a fire. Heller and Adler found that a piece of linen soaked in sulfuric acid for half an hour produced the requisite straw-yellow color of the Image. Light sources, including ultraviolet and infrared rays, gamma rays, and the other rays constituting the electromagnetic spectrum, were applied to linen—none produced the color of the Image. Furthermore, there was no evidence of any foreign substance (in anything like enough quantity) that could possibly be construed as being the result of painting, or rubbing, or spraying, or any conceivable artistic procedure. Spectroscopic analysis as well discovered no evidence of the metals which would have had to be present in any sort of inorganic "paint" that could make the image by artifice.

Reputable scientific conclusion #2:

THE IMAGE WAS FORMED BY DEHYDRATION AND OXIDATION OF THE FIBERS OF THE IMAGE AREA ITSELF, AND NOT BY ANY ADDED COLORING AGENT.

This is, so far, only to describe the chemical properties of the Image. There are a couple of other odd features which must be mentioned.

The various shades of color in the Image are not caused by a deeper or lighter coloring of any particular fibrils. They are caused rather by the density of colored fibrils in a given area. It is a lot like the half-tone prints in newspaper photos, where "black" is made by black ink dots bunched together, and "gray" is made by black ink dots interspersed with white areas. Suppose, then, that some sudden light or heat radiation mildly "scorched" the Shroud to make the Image. It is difficult to see how such a radiation could selectively produce the localized "on-off" coloring that produces the shading in the Image.

Nor could the Image be any sort of naturally produced oxidative scorch at all, since a scorch fluoresces orange under ultraviolet light, while the Image does not fluoresce at all. The only way the Image resembles a mild scorch is in its color and in its being the result of some kind of dehydration.

We must also recall that if the Image on the Shroud was somehow projected from the body by a kind of unknown "radiation" from that body, nothing could be natural about the process. Dead bodies do not radiate anything like what is required for the Image. Nor do they secrete any oils or vapors in any conceivable manner that could produce the undistorted 3-D detail of the Image.

The Image is a perfect three-dimensional rendition of a crucified man. Assuming the Shroud was in contact with the body, any transference of "something" from that body onto the Shroud, would, when the Shroud is straightened out, produce an utterly distorted Image. This is a point brought out strongly by John Jackson and other scientists who investigated the typography of transferring an image from a three dimensional object to a two dimensional object. Imagine rubbing your face with charcoal, and then pressing a cloth to it so that an image of your face would be transferred to the cloth. Then straighten out the cloth. Your nose, to take the most acutely three dimensional area as an example, would show up on the flattened cloth several times too wide. The imprint of your whole face would bloat laterally and longitudinally, making a comical distortion.

The Shroud Image, on the other hand, resembles exactly a mirror image. It is like the image you see when you look into a mirror face on. The mirror shows your whole frontal appearance in depth. It shows nothing of your sides, or the back side of your arms or legs, or the back of your head, or any of your head past the top point. If you turn your back to the mirror, though you can't see it, the image of your back would have the same characteristics. And in fact, this is exactly the portrait of the Crucified Man, front and back on the Shroud of Turin.

The most important thing to understand is that, supposing a radiation of some type proceeding outwards from every point on the body, if the Shroud that covers the body is draped or curved over it in any degree, the resulting image on the Shroud must necessarily be distorted. That holds especially if the source-points of the radiation throw out their rays in all directions. It also holds if the radiation proceeds straight outwards in single lines from every point on the body. And it also holds even if the "rays" were projected straight upwards to intersect the draped Shroud at an angle. No matter: once the Shroud is straightened out, it will have inscribed on it an image distorted to a degree that becomes more extreme as the curvature of the previously draped cloth was greater. It will be wider and a little longer than the original, and all the features on it will be wider and a bit longer. Most readers of this book have seen a reproduction of the Man on the Shroud. It is not the portrait of a roly-poly fellow with a face twice as wide as it is long. It is the spitting image of Near-Eastern Semitic male possibly in his thirties whose visage is serene and quietly majestic.

The only way, according to the optics of the situation, that the Image could be the mirror image that it is, is for the Shroud to have been stiff as a board as it lay atop the body. Then if any "rays" came straight upwards from the body, they would impact the Shroud so as to produce an undistorted image.

Reputable scientific conclusion #3:

NO ONE CAN TELL HOW THE IMAGE GOT ONTO THE SHROUD IN ORDER TO PRODUCE AN UNDISTORTED THREE-DIMENSIONAL COPY OF THE FRONT AND BACK OF THE BODY.

On the other hand, if we go back to the forgery thesis, we may say that of course the artist painted on a flat surface, producing an image faithful to his own conception. It would not be distorted. One may then ask how a medieval artist knew how to paint a pale, diffuse yellow image that disappears if you look at it close-up, and paint it in such a manner that a photographer (after photography was invented 600 years later), could take a picture of the Shroud, develop the negative, and watch as that negative suddenly and strikingly formed into a perfectly clear three dimensional image—an image not at all apparent from the original?

The photographer was Secondo Pia, and the year was 1898. In his own time Pia was accused of photographic fakery. He was not vindicated until Giuseppe Enrie duplicated his work in 1931, and again when Bill Mottern and John Jackson first produced their computerized image on a VP-8 Analyzer at Sandia Laboratory in Albuquerque in 1976.

John Heller, in the accompanying interview, tells us how this medieval magician would have had to work in order to acid-paint each individual microscopically-sized fibril. Recall that there is no "direction" that would be present even if a Pointillist applied tiny dots. Even a "dot" would betray a slight directional movement. Rather the color comes from acid-like degradation of the very crowns of individual micro-fibrils. And the micro-fibril next door might have no color. The "painting" would have to be done under a powerful microscope with an "enormous focal length" (notes Dr. Heller); and painted so fast that the acid would not destroy the artist's "brush"; and then immediately the artist would have to wash away the acid before it ate away the cloth—which would smear the image. And if he were to succeed in performing these impossible tasks, his "masterpiece" would look pale and flat and diffuse, only to come clear and distinct 600 years later in a photographic negative.

The further conclusion to reputable scientific conclusions 1, 2, and 3, is that what we have here is either a Medieval miracle or a first century miracle.

If the 1988 C14 test dates are correct, we have a Medieval miracle, complete with human (or at least primate) blood.

This is extremely important to understand. Walter McCrone and *Scientific American* notwithstanding, supposing that after all the C-14 tests performed in 1988 gave the true date, the fact is that the Image on the Shroud could not have been produced by any conceivable human agency—whatever the true date of the Shroud. If the Shroud were discovered today, and it was determined somehow that it was "made" today, it would still fail every scientific test intending to show that it could have been made by the hand of man.

If there was something wrong about the C-14 test, and the correct date is around 33 A.D., we have overwhelming indications that the Turin Shroud is the authentic burial cloth of Jesus Christ, with an oxidation Image faithfully reproducing his features—either as a by-product of the Resurrection, or as a purposeful supernatural work done at the time of the Resurrection, for a sign and an aid to belief. In either case, it is worth remarking that it was twentieth century science that first demonstrated the detailed chemistry and 3-D optics of the Shroud, and ruefully declared it could not conceive of how the Image could possibly have gotten onto the cloth. And it was nineteenth and twentieth century skeptical theology that began to question the literal truth of the Resurrection.

THE 1988 C14 TEST OF THE SHROUD

The remaining problem is the C14 date that places the origin of the Shroud most probably in the latter part of the 13th century. To understand how the date can be wrong, we must know a little bit about radiocarbon dating. C14 dating was developed during the 1940s by Willard F. Libby. (Libby's *Radiocarbon Dating*, Second Edition, 1955, is still worth reading to learn the theory and early methodology of C14 dating.) C14 is a radioactive isotope of normal Carbon, C12. It is manufactured in the atmosphere by cosmic rays which knock into Nitrogen atoms to produce the isotope. Theoretically, the influx of cosmic rays into the atmosphere surrounding the earth is fairly constant. The result is that the amount of C14 produced in the world is fairly constant. Plants ingest carbon dioxide directly and animals indirectly by eating plants. Living things consume C14 along with C12, and these both become built into the body. While they are alive, they take in new C14 as the C14 they already have begins to decay radioactively. But when they die, they consume no new C14, while the C14 they contain continues to decay. All of this in turn means that any newly dead plant or animal, at any given historical moment, will start off with a theoretically similar ratio of C12 to C14. This C14 will decay rapidly at first, and then more slowly, according to an exponential curve translating into a half-life calculated these days as around 5730 years.

You can then measure the rate of C14 decay per unit weight. The faster that decay, the more recently the plant or animal died. As the carbon sample gets older, the decay of C14 will slow down. A formula has been derived that can judge the age of a piece of carbon on the basis of its present rate of radioactive decay. The mechanical details of the operation are complex and are under constant revision. A recently developed technique, which was used by the three labs in the 1988 radiocarbon test of the Shroud, goes under the name of "accelerator mass spectrometry." But no matter what technique is used, the formulas applied always depend on a constant ratio of C12 to C14 in the atmosphere. Only then can a "C14 clock" starting at 1000 A.D. be comparable to one starting at 500 A.D.

In fact cosmic rays are not quite constant over any given historical period. There are short cycles that are thought to be connected to sun spot cycles, there are longer cycles lasting hundreds of years, and there are many inexplicable glitches and bumps during some historical periods. All of this variation means that the C12 to C14 ratio that starts the radiocarbon "clock" will vary, and throw off the results of a C14 test.

Another form of dating is done by counting tree rings. Each tree ring translates to one year, as a tree grows in the spring and summer and stops growing in the fall and winter, producing a dark, narrow ring in contrast to the lighter and wider growth patterns. The science of dating by counting tree rings is called dendrochronology. A good deal of recent work in this science has been accomplished with the use of the bristlecone pine, a tree that lives 3000 years or more, and which is found in the desert regions of the Western United States. Similar work has been done on sequoias and, in Europe, on oak trees and firs. Ideally a cross-section of the trunk of a very old tree provides a perfect mapping of time. The center of the trunk should radiocarbon test very old, in the first years of the tree's existence. Each step outwards should produce younger dates, until the outermost rings should test to the time when the tree was chopped down.

But it was found that there is always a discrepancy between the tree-ring date and the radiocarbon date. The discrepancy varies consistently with the age of the tree. What is the cause of the discrepancy? No one knows for sure, but it is suggested that a variation in atmospheric C14 will throw off test dates from one era to another. Since tree-ring dates are held to be certain, a correction curve has been established to bring the less certain C14 dates into harmony with tree ring dates. Every raw C14 date performed on any carbonated material—charcoal, wood, linen, ashes—is thus "corrected" by the formula derived from tree-ring dates.

There is, however, no standardized correction curve as yet that has the acceptance of the great majority of scientists involved in radiocarbon dating. It is still a matter of testing and retesting, and constant revising on the basis of new data.

Furthermore the *theory* behind the correction curve relies on the assumption that radioactive decay in trees is directly comparable to radioactive decay in any other carbonated materials—such as charcoal or linen. Is this the case? We will touch on this problem a bit later when we talk about "biofractionation."

The dendrochronological correction had an interesting effect on the Shroud dating. The youngest raw date came from the Arizona lab. Figuring in the plus-or-minus error factor, the date comes out at 1390 A.D. The oldest raw date comes from Oxford. Adding in the error factor, the corresponding date was 1090 A.D. The range here is 300 years, with a mean date of 1240 A.D. But after "calibration" (correction by the tree-ring scale), the calendar dates range from 1210 to 1410, a later span with a smaller range. In the actual report published in the British science journal *Nature* (16 February 1989), a good deal of statistical manipulation was performed. This averaging arrived at a final range of 1260 to 1390 A.D., with the higher probability towards the earlier date. The actual mean figure for the three labs (at a 68% confidence level) is 1281 A.D. We can see, however, that the raw results, involving direct counting of C14 decay, had a pretty wide range. These results may show a variation of the C12\C14 ratio within the samples themselves, and thus some probable contamination.

The widely reported "95% chance that the Shroud was made between 1260 and 1390 A.D." sounds impressive, but it is the result of statistical sleight-of-hand. A reported 68% chance that the true date lies within a given range represents one "standard deviation." It is based on a standard statistical formula applied to the number of, and scattered results of, "runs" in a dating procedure. Plus and minus years are plugged in to signify the possible deviation from the true date. The plus and minus years are then widened to arrive at two "standard deviations," establishing (it is said) a 95% chance that the true date lies within this widened range.

It all amounts to internal massaging of numbers which hides certain warning signals. In fact the wide range of dates among the three labs obtained in the Shroud sample as compared to the much narrower range in the three control samples indicates that the Shroud test gave an anomalous result. The report in *Nature* hints at the problem when it notes (in Table 2) that there is only a 5% probability of attaining by chance "a scatter among the three dates as high as that observed, under the assumption that the quoted errors reflect all sources of random variation." In plain English this means that all the statistical manipulation in the world can't get rid of the fact that the range of dates is much too large to be accounted for by the expected errors built into radiocarbon dating.

To put it another way: there is a 95 out of 100% chance that the discrepancy in the raw dates means that there were variable ratios of $C12$ and $C14$ in the samples themselves.

And since the samples were taken from the same tiny area, the range of dates most probably means that all you have to do is go one or two millimeters up the sample, closer to a scorch mark, or perhaps within an area containing a restoration thread or two, to throw off your results a couple of hundred years or more—perhaps much more.

What brings much greater doubt into the picture is a radiocarbon test performed at the University of California in 1982. Dr. Heller sent a sample from the Shroud to the nuclear accelerator lab there. It was a single thread. One end tested to 200 A.D., the other to 1000 A.D., or, according to Dr. Adler, 1200 A.D. The early date, that of 200 A.D., with an added "error," has been grabbed onto by partisans to claim it means the Shroud is truly of Jesus's time. Unfortunately no such claim can be made. The test was run by a scientist with no great experience in the field. The thread had starch on one end, and we do not even know if it was the starched end that tested earlier. The thread was not treated to rid it of surface contaminants. The dates were not dendrochronologically corrected and no statistical analysis was performed. All things considered, two dates from a single thread 800 or 1000 years apart mean not that you can choose one date and go away happy, but that the test itself is flawed beyond any and all validity. The results of that test mean you must throw out the test.

However, we mention this 1982 radiocarbon test to suggest that contamination, known or unknown, can skew C14 dates radically. It throws into vivid relief the axiom that supreme care must be taken to make sure the sample you are testing is truly representative of the original living plant.

The theory of radiocarbon dating assumes that the ratio of C12 to C14 will be equal throughout the object dated. If that is not so, the whole procedure is discredited. There are many examples of radically divergent dates obtained by radiocarbon analysis. In one such case—one of many—radiocarbon dating was performed on a primitive Alaskan settlement. Hearth charcoal was dated, and wooden posts that had been a part of the houses were tested. Archaeologists had determined, by standard stratigraphical methods, that the wooden posts were at least nearly the same age as the charcoal. But radiocarbon dating gave a date range of 1800 to 1550 B.C. for the charcoal, and a range of 1000 to 800 B.C. for the posts. What is the answer to this 700 to 1000 year discrepancy? A mixture of charcoal and wood at the same site dated to about half-way in between; obviously it was something about the wood and the charcoal themselves that made for the different results. What was it? There is no answer. More theoretical and experimental work should be undertaken to determine why different carbonated materials from the same location can sometimes give vastly different radiocarbon dates. Could carbon compounds have seeped into the wooden posts over the centuries? Could it be that carbon exchange had occurred? Or biofractionation?

Drs. Dmitri Kouznetsov and Andrey Ivanov, colleagues at the Sedov Biopolymer Research Laboratory in Moscow, have recently performed a series of experiments in which they duplicated, as nearly as possible, the conditions of the 1532 fire that came close to destroying the Shroud. Conditions were hot enough, around 960 degrees Celsius, to melt silver—some silver droplets were found on the Shroud. Water was tossed on the silver cask containing the Shroud to douse the fire. Since some of that water got into the cask and stained the Shroud in various places, we know that the cask was not watertight and not airtight.

The two Russian scientists consulted fire prevention experts in France and in Russia in order to determine the concentrations of carbon dioxide and carbon monoxide that would result from combustion during a fire, these being gases from outside sources (the tapestries and burning walls) that would be in the immediate vicinity of the Shroud. They added steam and molten silver to the mix. Steam and carbon dioxide, catalyzed by the presence of silver ions, would produce large amounts of carbonic acid. This acid in turn easily bonds to the OH radicals in the cellulose of the linen, forming very strong molecular links. The experiment concluded that up to 20% of the carbon in the cellulose would have undergone exchange with this new carbon during the fire.

The two scientists utilized experimental conditions of 140 degrees Celsius and durations of from one to twelve hours. In later experiments they raised the temperature to 200 and then 300 degrees. The real 1532 fire lasted (it is thought) about six hours, and reached temperatures of at least 900 degrees C. in the vicinity of the silver cask. Dr. Ray Rogers, one of the original STURP team members, had investigated the thermal conditions of the fire back in the 1970s and had decided on a temperature of around 200 degrees Celsius inside the silver cask. Kouznetsov seems to have reached nearly the same conclusions, and seems satisfied with the 20% figure given by the 200-300 degree temperature. The 20% figure for carbon exchange translates to an age twice as old as that given by the labs that tested the Shroud. It would push the date back to around 600 or 700 A.D. (A 40% exchange would push the true date back to the first century.)

Kouznetsov has also been looking into biofractionation

as a possible cause for a further date correction. It turns out that the various compounds in a flax plant contain different concentrations of C14. The highest concentration is in the cellulose, with lesser amounts in the lipids, proteins, and nucleic acids.

During the manufacture of linen from flax, it undergoes (up until very recent times) a process called retting. The flax fibers are soaked in water to ferment. Eventually bacteria eat away most of the other constituents of the flax, leaving approximately 98% pure cellulose. This remainder is what the linen is woven from. Linen is therefore not representative of the flax plant as a whole, and with its higher concentration of C14, it will test too young.

Another source of error being investigated by the Russians is the normal alkalization that occurs to textiles (and other wood products) over time. This is the process that yellows linen with age. But alkalization produces methyls and carboxyls, again distorting the dating results. This would mean that the older the sample, the more probable that it would test too young by radiocarbon dating. Could something like this have accounted for the more recent date given by the wood in the Alaskan radiocarbon analysis in the example discussed above?

According to a videotaped presentation at the Turin Shroud Center of Colorado last year, Kouznetsov estimates that carbon exchange during the 1532 fire, combined with biofractionation in the flax plant, should provide corrections to the laboratory tests that would date the Shroud to the first century A.D.

The problem is that biofractionation and alkalization should skew the results of any radiocarbon tests on linen. But one of the control samples dated by the three labs in 1988 was a piece of mummy cloth from Cleopatra's time. And Cleopatra's time was very near Jesus's time. Here the labs achieved a pretty close hit, as they did on the other two control samples (both of these were from Medieval times). Only if the mummy cloth had been preserved under much different conditions than the Shroud could alkalization have much of a differential effect. And biofractionation in the living flax plant would apply to all linen tested, of whatever age.

Which brings us back to the Shroud fire. Dr. Adler points out that the 40% carbon exchange supposedly needed to push the date back to the first century need not be so. A much lesser percentage is needed if another type of kinetic isotope effect, not from the biology of living plants, but from chemical reactions during the fire, took place. It would have the same result as biofractionation in the flax plant, but would produce differential C14 production chemically and not biologically. A higher ratio of C14 would obtain during the carbon exchange, with the result that, say, a 20% exchange could mean a first century date. But the quantities and the conditions of the fire are not knowable with any degree of reliability, as Dr. Adler is quick to point out. The fire is however the most promising event to look for revised C14 dates. At least in the Shroud fire we have a discernable chemical reaction that would have occurred in the mixture of combustion gases, steam and silver ions.

The sample taken for the 1988 tests was on the border of

a repair strip. These strips were sewn into the Shroud to mend the areas that had been damaged by the fire. They contained linen that had probably been manufactured somewhere around 1532 A.D. The piece of cloth that was cut for the sample was seen to have a bit of this new cloth in it. So it was cut smaller to get rid of the repair cloth. No one bothered to see if any threads from the new cloth remained in the sample. A video of the sampling process exists: that process, according to Dr. Adler, was a scientific disaster.

The sample was taken from an area near a scorch, and near the border of a water stain. In these areas especially some volatile chemistry occurred during the intense heat, the water turned to steam, the production of silver ions and combustion gases, and all the other reactions we can only guess at. As Dr. Adler says, it was a thoroughly stupid place on the Shroud from which to take the sample, and it is not as if the people who took the sample had not been warned that the C14 dates could be radically skewed in this area of the Shroud. The videotape of the sample-taking shows two textile experts arguing for an hour over the site.

Radiocarbon dating is not magic. Even when the lab work is first rate, everything depends on the purity and uniformity of the sample, to make sure the C14 clock starts at the right place. We can hypothesize that the fire conditions, the carbon exchange, along with the other chemistry, and perhaps the presence of new cloth, all combined to skew the C14 results by 1300 years.

There is another possibility to account for radically wrong dates. Every other indication points to the Shroud as being the genuine burial cloth of Jesus Christ. Forensic evidence has been painstakingly developed to demonstrate that the aspect of the body and the pattern of the blood conform to a real crucifixion. There is evidence of scourge marks on the back and legs (about 120 of them), wounds from a crown of thorns, and a lance wound in the side. Some of the scourge marks appear only under ultraviolet light—a fact which would necessitate a forger to "paint" the marks so that they would be invisible to the naked eye, and (by means of black magic perhaps), discern that ultraviolet equipment would be invented some 650 years later.

The visage is that of a pure type of Near-Eastern Semite. Pollen has been discovered on the Shroud which is found in the Near East but not in Europe. All indications conform to the Gospel accounts of the Crucifixion, and the Image points to the Resurrection.

The alternative hypothesis is that the Resurrection may have been accompanied by neutron radiation. (Neutrons are what cosmic rays are made of.) According to this theory, massive amounts of C14 would have been implanted in the Shroud as a by-product of the Resurrection. In effect, the very process that made the Image could have kicked the C14 clock ahead 1300 years. Or maybe only 650 years, if the chemical reactions during the fire kicked it ahead another 650 years. By such a combination of events—a neutron shower during the Resurrection, and a carbon exchange during the fire—we may arrive at a corrected radiocarbon date of c. 33 A.D. However, we know that the fire occurred, and that a carbon exchange would have occurred in the fire, but we can't know if a Resurrection neutron shower occurred.

Believers know by Faith and by the historical account in the Gospels that Jesus Christ was resurrected. The Resurrection was a supernatural event. We simply do not know what possible natural effects this supernatural event could have produced. It could have produced "supernatural rays," or a neutron shower, or anything that could have kicked ahead the C14 clock. And it also could have purposefully imprinted an oxidation copy of the body on the Shroud. But if the Resurrection itself skewed the C14 clock, there is no area of the Shroud that would test true.

OPTICS & ENIGMAS

Why do I favor a purposefully made imprint and not some sort of automatic by-product of the Resurrection?

The most intriguing mystery about the Shroud is the 3-D negative image that remained undistorted. Recall the mirror analogy. If the mirror you look into is uneven, or curved as fun house mirrors are, the image that stares back at you will be distorted. The curvature of the mirror is just like the drape of the cloth over the body. You simply cannot account for a true image without a flat mirror or a flat Shroud. Dr. John Jackson, one of the original STURP team members, has wracked his brain for 20 years trying to come up with an answer. Suppose, he says, the Shroud literally passed through the body at the moment of the Resurrection. Previously draped over the corpse, in contact with the nose, the brow, the chest, the feet, and other protruding parts of the body, it now straightens and flattens, imprinting on itself the image of the rest of the body in an undistorted manner. The prominent features will have imprinted earlier and longer, the overall effect giving the color gradations that contain the 3-D information that comes clear in a negative print.

Such a hypothesis sounds incredible on the face of it, but Jackson is forced into this reasoning by the optics of the Shroud Image. He claims to have come up with the mathematics that would fit his scenario. As we have seen, any draping or curvature of the Shroud would necessarily distort any straight-line or globally scattered radiation that went from the surface of the body to the Shroud.

But one suspects this is pushing natural science too far. If we must posit a cloth passing through the body, we have already violated physical laws. We can never know exactly what happened during the Resurrection act. We can imagine as a part of that act, a spiritualized body that, just before it disappeared to once again reappear outside the tomb, intentionally blasted a portrait of itself on the cloth. Complete with selectively localized coloring that would project a 3-D effect on a photographic plate 1900 years in the future.

On the other hand, Dr. Jackson's hypothesis, incredible as it seems, gains some force if we recall the appearances of the Resurrected Christ. According to the Gospels, that "Spiritual Body" could appear and disappear at will. Perhaps it was that Spiritual Body, crossing the line between the physical and the supernatural, that became "like air" and allowed the Shroud to pass through it from face and chest to back and underside of the legs, during that process imprinting an undistorted Image on the burial cloth.

But to my mind, there is more of a sense of the supernatural throughout the whole process of Image-making. The only natural thing about it is the effect, which is that oxidized coloring which produced the Shroud image.

This is especially so since the Image contains astounding 3-D information *which could not have been discerned until photography was invented.* A skeptic could say that such a seemingly forward-looking intention is merely the fortuitous result of the process of Imaging. The rejoinder is that the process of Imaging itself necessarily goes beyond physics and beyond nature. There is so much about the Shroud that seems intended for the 20th century. When the Shroud was discovered (or rather re-discovered) in the mid-fourteenth century, many Churchmen called it a forgery. Only chemical testing like that performed by Heller and Adler could demonstrate beyond a doubt that the Shroud is *not* a forgery. Only in recent times have chemical tests been developed that could testify to the presence of blood from tiny samples. And how providential was it that a sophisticated piece of equipment developed in the late 20th century to enhance the clarity of space photos would be turned on the Shroud with such astonishing results? Why did the only people in the world who had access to a VP-8 Analyzer suddenly become interested in the Shroud?

There is a further enigma. The blood on the Shroud must have gotten there by contact with the corpse—while it remained a corpse. (In fact Dr. Heller ascertained that the blood got on the Shroud before the Image. Fibrils in the Image area that had been covered by blood were not colored. Whatever made the Image did not go through the blood to the Shroud.)

At the time the blood got on the Shroud, the Shroud must have been draped and curved naturally in conformity with the high and low areas of the body. It should have therefore formed a distorted pattern that would be out of synch with the undistorted Image. But the pattern of the blood seems to conform to the pattern of the Image. It drips from wounds in the forehead. It drips down the arms. It clings around the edges of the scourge marks on the back and legs.

Dr. Jackson has however discerned a distortion pattern in some areas of the blood, especially a mass of blood that seems to be implanted in the hair at the sides of the face. The blood in the uppermost places (on the forehead, say, or on the top surface of the arm) would not be distorted. Nor would the blood from the scourge marks be noticeably distorted, since they are each small in area, and most appear on the fairly flat surfaces of the back and chest. But blood on the side of the face and the side of the chest should be distorted laterally. Here is an area that would seem to call for more examination. One must look for blood distortion patterns on the sides of every curved portion of the corpse where blood is present. But perhaps this is easier said than done, and Dr. Jackson's work in this area may be as complete as can be humanly accomplished.

We can surmise the intentional reason (if it is such) for the chemistry of the coloring that made the Image. Oxidative degradation of the fibrils is the chemical mechanism. That acid-like imprint has withstood all the ravages of time. It withstood extreme heat in the 1532 fire that would have made any pigments or gelatin run and bake into different colors. It has withstood numerous washings and scrubbings and starchings, and all the bacteria and mites that could have attacked it. It remained intact while over the ages hundreds of devout people kissed it and touched objects to it, and painters pressed their works to it, and scorches were burnt into it.

Dr. Adler points to a twentieth century concern. Since the chemistry of the Image is the same as an acid degradation, this century's acidic atmospheric pollution will color the cloth until it matches the color of the Image, and make it disappear as a discernable Image. The Image will not get darker to keep pace, since the coloring is "saturated": it is as dark as it will ever get. That is the nature of the chemical reaction.

It is certainly cause for concern. Is it a mystery of time? The twentieth century first gave us a look at a 3-D negative photograph, which shows us just what Our Lord looked like when He walked the earth. The twentieth century gave us the technology to let scientists tell us that science is unable to disauthenticate the Shroud. It is twentieth century science that by implication has verified a miracle.

And the twentieth century poisoned the air to place the Shroud in the kind of jeopardy it has not encountered in twenty centuries.

PART II

THE INTERVIEW
WITH HELLER AND ADLER

John H. Heller received a doctorate in medicine from Case Western Reserve. He taught internal medicine and medical physics at Yale, and later established the New England Institute, for research in biophysics and chemistry. In 1983 he published a book, Report on the Shroud of Turin, *that remains the very best popular scientific account of the Shroud. He died just before this book went to press. Alan D. Adler received a doctorate at the University of Pennsylvania, where he later taught molecular biology. He is now emeritus professor of chemistry at Western Connecticut State University. His chief work is in the field of biophysical chemistry. Since 1978 both scientists had been deeply involved in chemical and biophysical research on the Shroud of Turin.*

47

Dr. John Heller looks on as Joan Janney examines Shroud fibrils through a sophisticated microscope at the Air Force Academy in Colorado Springs.

Dr. Alan Adler also examining Shroud fibrils at the Air Force Academy. This was at a special conference called by STURP leaders John Jackson and Eric Jumper to test the microchemistry of the Shroud.

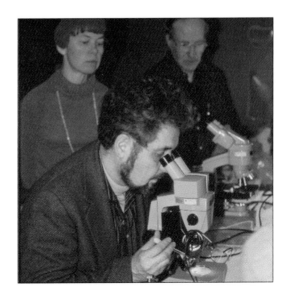

The Setting

I drove up from Washington, D.C. to Connecticut with some excitement, since I was finally to meet and talk with the author of *Report on the Shroud of Turin*. This is a popular scientific account of the STURP team's 1978 trip to Italy, the near disasters and last minute successes of that journey, and the follow-up meetings, experiments and fierce contentions surrounding the question of how the Shroud was made. Most importantly it documents in detail the chemical work that determined the real characteristics of the Image. The book is a classic of scientific discovery, told with humor and filled with the foibles of human nature. The interview took place in Dr. Heller's apartment. I was at first saddened to see that the biochemist was not in the best of health. He was confined to a wheel chair. In a few moments Dr. Adler rapped on the door and joined us. I am thankful for Adler's unexpected appearance, since John Heller was so obviously a sick man. I had begun to think it would be a huge burden on him to answer questions for two or three hours. I had been thinking of cutting the interview short, with just a question or two, a statement of gratitude for Dr. Heller's work, and then I would go away and leave the man in peace.

That was not to be. Dr. Adler quickly took the lead, and the three of us ended up talking hour after hour, with John Heller interjecting comments, sometimes piquant, always to the point.

The conditions were not the best. I had a tiny cassette recorder which I put on the coffee table. The maid came in and started running a vacuum cleaner. We moved out to the second-story porch, where it rained off and on, and the sound of traffic going by sometimes drowned our words. We ended up almost knee to knee around a tiny round metal table, heads bent together as if we were secretly conspiring to overthrow the cosmos. I am eternally grateful for both scientists' graciousness, and their concern to answer my sometimes naive questions with verve and an ultimate tribute to scientific accuracy.

When a reporter tapes an interview, he later transcribes it and then sends the transcript back to the person interviewed for approval and editing. Thank God Dr. Adler performed this task: the rough draft I sent him contained an awful lot of [garbled . . . garbled] and [spelling? . . . spelling?]. And he changed nothing that he had said or that Dr. Heller had said. It is refreshing to talk to scientists. At their best, they are loyal to the truth of things large and small.

Here's the way it went. And, I must add, the interview is the most valuable part of this book. It is two chemists, distilling 15 years of experience, with no holds barred.

TRANSCRIPT OF THE INTERVIEW

Case: Neither of you were original members of STURP, the Shroud of Turin Research Project composed mostly of American scientists, who investigated the Shroud in 1978, nor did you make the trip to Italy with the team. However, Dr. Heller's 1983 book, *Report on the Shroud of Turin,* is far-and-away the best piece of scientific writing I have read on the subject. What first piqued your interest in the Shroud?

Dr. Heller: It's a mystery. It's an unanswered question that should lend itself to scientific verification. I read the article by Barbara Culliton in *Science.* Where she was talking about the physics of miracles. [*Science,* vol. 201, 21 July 1978]

Case: Your book recounts a series of experiments you and Dr. Adler performed which proved beyond question that the blood on the Shroud is really blood, and that the straw-yellow image was formed by a dehydrative oxidation of the topmost fibrils of the linen.

Dr. Heller: Yes.

Case: Your experiments have withstood the severest scientific peer review. How do you answer Dr. Walter McCrone's still-current claim that the so-called blood is really vermillion paint (made from mercuric sulfide) and that the image was painted with a gelatin-based medium speckled with particles of red ochre (which is made from iron oxide)?

<u>Dr. Adler</u>: Actually that reprint I gave you answers this well. [J.H. Heller and A.D. Adler, "A Chemical Investigation of the Shroud of Turin," *Canadian Society for Forensic Science Journal,* vol. 14, No. 3, 1981.] We pointed out that yes, we saw what Walter claimed he saw. We saw iron oxide, we saw one piece of vermillion, we saw protein. We also saw red particles that weren't iron oxide. We might as well deal with that right now. The red we saw was blood, and it was in the blood tape samples from Turin; the only places we saw iron oxide was in the water stain areas and the blood scorch areas. And our explanation is, when you burn blood you get iron oxide—it contains iron.

We gave a mechanism why the iron should be expected to be found in the water stain areas. Because the iron is bound to this type of retted linen, and water from dousing the fire formed iron oxide by a series of simple reactions—and we tested it by experiment, and found it was the only way to explain the presence of iron inside the lumen of the fibers.

The vermillion is easily explained. We only saw it once; he [McCrone] maybe saw it once too. But we know that there were artists who painted reproductions of the Shroud; we discovered, talking to Shroud scholars and in some books on the Shroud, that very frequently these artists sanctified their paintings by pressing them up against the original. And so we wouldn't be surprised to find the artist's pigments on the Shroud, which he claimed he saw, and we saw some of also. But that doesn't prove that it's everywhere.

On the other hand, x-ray results make it very clear that in fact the blood can't be composed of mercuric sulfide. And the reason is very simple. If you've ever seen an x-ray of tooth fillings, the mercury stands out. You can't "see" the blood in the x-rays. If the blood were 1/3 cinnabar like McCrone claims, the mercury would show up on the x-ray studies, and it doesn't.

As to the gelatin, we ran some very sensitive tests for proteins [gelatin contains proteins]—and we found out that we could not detect any protein in the image area. The only place we could detect protein was in the blood areas. McCrone claims it's in the image area, on the basis of a microscopic observation—and so it's not up to us to answer him. It's up to him to answer us, in a certain sense. We simply asked and tested more questions than he did.

I might point something else out. Some of the experiments that were done on the spectroscopy on the site [in Turin in 1978] were, well, not the fancy quality we could expect from today's instrumentation—in an experiment designed to really get the spectra. They were low resolution, low sensitivity, with the instruments they borrowed, but they did what they did. But while you might say, hey, they weren't of the highest quality—once we had some idea of what to look for and where, the spectroscopy of the Shroud is in agreement with our microscopic studies and not with McCrone's.

If there were protein in the image area—you can actually see the amide 1,2,3 bands in the infrared of the blood areas; you don't see it in the infrared of the image area. And so while there are poor quality spectra, the macroscopic data is in agreement with the microscopic data. Ours, not his.

<u>Case</u>: So you can be certain that the Shroud is not the work of an artist?

<u>Dr. Adler</u>: Well, I will not say it isn't an artist; I can only say it isn't a painter. But the other thing you can point out is, that Dr. John Jackson has tested somewhere on the order of twenty different types of artistic rendition techniques by VP-8 experiments. And they don't give the same quality of image that the Shroud does. And therefore those techniques can also be ruled out.

So, I can't say there was no insanely clever artist in history who developed some technique by which he could make the Shroud. I can say, if he did, he didn't do it by any of the twenty techniques that Jackson tested.

<u>Dr. Heller</u>: And it's not a forgery. The image is only one fiber thick. It does not penetrate beyond the surface of the thread. In order to paint just a tiny fibril—I liken them to the hair on your arm—those microfibrils—you'd have to have a micromanipulator, and a microscope with an enormous focal length, so you could see from a distance, and paint each hair individually, and then know how many hairs to paint, so you get a photographic negative, which would develop.

Case: Pretty neat trick.

Dr. Heller: Very neat trick.

Case: Let's move on to some questions that I myself wanted some answers to. Let's start with the blood. Would you go over the evidence that makes you certain that the blood on the Shroud is really blood?

Dr. Adler: Well there's a whole table you have reference to [in the article Drs. Heller and Adler published in *Canadian Society for Forensic Science Journal,* vol. 14, No. 3 (1981)]. The fact is, it meets a lot of the test criteria, by color changes; it has the right kind of spectra; the microspectra, the macrospectra; it meets the descriptions that were required by the medical people, as to what it should look like. But the most interesting thing is now there is immunological evidence that it is primate blood. There are previous tests by an Italian by the name of Bollone. He tested it, but he tested it for blood type, and he found AB, because a lot of old materials test AB—because it can be confused with bacterial cell-wall contamination. You get immunological tests for two reasons: the proteins have stretches of sugars, so-called saccharides that the common blood antibodies react to. And cell walls of bacteria are in fact saccharides. Now, a lot of proteins are glycoproteins. It turns out that common blood antigens for ABO types are glycoproteins, and so the test is based on the sugar determinant. The test *I* ran, was for albumin, which is a more specific immunological test, for the simple reason that it's a pure peptide. You're looking for protein structure only, not confusing saccharides. We got a positive test for albumin. But you can only run this test as a surface test.

Case: How do you mean a surface test?

Dr. Adler: Well, you put it on, you tag the antibody with some fluorescent tag so you can see if it sticks to the surface you are putting it on. See if it lights up. And, that's not the world's best immunological test. We found out that a chimp antigen gave almost as strong a test. So our conclusion was a very simple one. We were only willing to say it was a primate's blood. But we were not willing at that point to declare it was human blood. Like we tell talk show audiences, if you choose to think that the image you see is that of a chimp or an orangutan, you're perfectly welcome to believe that.

Case: But there hasn't been more recent testing that is specific for human blood? Or can that be done, actually?

Dr. Adler: Well it could be. But you'd need more sample. And the ultimate test would be DNA testing. It hasn't been done. There's been one claim, again by one of the Italians, and I don't know whether I believe it.

Case: Why is the blood red, or reddish, instead of black or dark brown?

<u>Dr. Adler</u>: Yeah. Well, a lot of people thought the blood we see in mummies is black, but they don't realize that's because you've got a thick amount of blood. If you look at a thin section of it, you'd see it was brown. And in fact this is sort of interesting. The fact that the blood is red, is an independent piece of evidence that this is, in fact, a severely beaten man whose image is on that cloth. One of the surprising things about the chemical evidence we collected on the blood is that there is a very high amount of one of the blood break-down products, bilirubin. When you break red blood cells, like when you beat somebody, or when you subject him to severe traumatic shock, the hemoglobin goes through the liver, and what the liver does, is to take the broken blood cells, the hemoglobin from those, and converts it to what are called bile pigments: biliverdin and eventually bilirubin for excretion. So bilirubin is frequently tested—this is the stuff that makes jaundice, when you clinically test for evidence of broken blood cells, and those sorts of things.

So that's a blood-derived breakdown product, and we saw bilirubin. We saw a lot of it. The reason why that blood is red—it took a lot of years of argument among some of us who worked on the Shroud to understand what we were saying. John [Heller] and I said it's an exudate from a clot, and Gil Lavoie said it's an exudate from a clot. It's only after we argued about it for about four years that we finally understood what we meant. When blood clots, like a wound here, you see around the edge of the wound, there is serum, squeezed out around it. The clot contracts because of the fibrin in it. And it squeezes out the serum. That serum, the exudate, has excess albumin in it, and it has a small amount of hemoglobin, and the albumin carries all the bilirubin that's there. All right? So what you've got on the exudate of the clot, is in fact a blood-derived protein mixture where you've increased the ratio of bilirubin to hemoglobin, over what you'd see in normal blood. And that's interesting, because when blood dries out, the protein changes its structure. And the spectrum of the hemoglobin changes to give you a sort of reddish-brown color, the brown color, that happens to oxidized blood—you're right, when blood ages this color change takes place. But bilirubin is yellow-orange. Especially when it's bound on the protein. And if you mix the two, what do you get? You get red.

And so the fact that the blood is red, and still red, is proof of the fact that this is blood from a man who died a very traumatic death. Which is in agreement with the pathological image evidence.

<u>Case</u>: Is the blood pretty much the same color all over the Shroud?

<u>Dr. Adler</u>: No, there are some places where the blood in fact is darker. For example, from the scourge marks.

<u>Case</u>: How about the serum areas? They're lighter, I guess?

<u>Dr. Adler</u>: There are some serum areas that are lighter. In fact, one of the things that's interesting: around each of the scourge marks, and around the lance wound mark, if you

look under ultraviolet, you actually see this serum exudate. Because that serum exudate fluoresces. You can actually see a border line around each area. You have to ask yourself, (1) how could an artist know to paint that? And (2) to be able to paint it, he'd have to paint seeing in ultraviolet light. He'd have to do it for every single blood mark on the cloth. There's what, 120 scourge marks as I remember?

Dr. Heller: There are over 100.

Case: In general, how does the pattern and chemistry of the blood conform to forensic evidence indicating a crucifixion?

Dr. Adler: Well, there's a whole book on that by Monsignor Ricci. What he's done, is to explore the patterns the blood flows take. Paul Vignon did this too, around 1900. The blood marks you see in the arms look strange for the way the arms are in the image, but they are not strange if you remember he was originally in a crucifixion position, so the blood would flow down the arm. Which is what it looks like it does . . .

Case: Which is what it does . . .

Dr. Adler: Yeah. On the other hand, you look at a lot of scourge marks, and they also look as if these were made on a man who was bent over being scourged and then put upright. Because some start this way [gestures] and then start going this way [gestures]. And Ricci has explored every single one of those and shown that they in fact conform to what you'd expect on a man who had been flogged and crucified, and he asked "where's the flow patterns?" And he's looked into that in great detail in a huge thick book, which is originally in Italian, and I believe there's an English translation as well.

<u>Case</u>: You and Dr. Heller performed exhaustive tests to find out what could have made the image. After two years of testing, you found that diimide, a potent reducing agent, turned a yellow fibril pure white. This was in effect the reverse of the image-making process. At that point you could be sure that the "image maker" involved the opposite of reduction, i.e., oxidation. Could you explain further the chemical tests and conclusions you came to? You don't have to go into the whole chemistry of it . . .

<u>Dr. Adler</u>: The most important thing was, we tested for all the things that might have had the yellow, red, orange, and brown colors, known from medieval pigments, inorganic and organic, and they all gave negative tests. We also tried to extract the color, with a huge range of solvents. We couldn't extract it. We found on the other hand that strong oxidation and strong reduction got rid of the color. We also found that if we took present day linen fibers, and we oxidized them, they gave the Shroud image color. This suggested that the color was a direct change of the chemical structure of the cellulose, not an applied pigment. All right. What happens when you start oxidizing something? You get all kinds of reactions. If you carry them out under different conditions you

get different kinds of structures. And we found that the one that came closest to what we were seeing was the color that we described in the paper [published in 1981 in the Canadian journal], and accounted for the color on the Shroud too.

I would also point out again, the spectroscopy on the Shroud is consistent with this chemical testing, both the ultraviolet spectroscopy and the infrared spectroscopy. And if you're not sure this can happen, as we used to tell audiences, ask any housewife, what happens to dirty linen after you let it sit around for a year or two, even in a drawer. It turns yellow.

You can look at various things that catalyze this type of chemistry, to speed up the reaction. Alkali is very slow and doesn't give as strong a yellow color as quickly as acid.

When we say this yellow color is due to a particular kind of chemical structure, we're not talking about a single chemical compound. Cellulose is a polymer. And so we're saying that there are a variety of chemical structures there, and there are several chemical paths that produce the structure that we claim leads to the color. Now the one thing they've all got in common is, it's a whole series of different oxidative type reactions. When you eventually oxidize cellulose you produce an acidic structure. So, its very logical that after the reaction goes for a bit, it's going to be acid catalyzed. The reason we think it's an oxidation is, no matter how you get there, a reduction will reverse all of them. So that was the point of the diimide test. Now we actually tried some of these other sources to see what kind of oxidation they produced, as well as looking in the literature. Ultra-violet light did not produce this type of oxidation. It produced an oxidized material that wasn't yellow. Infrared also won't do it. Alkaline reactions tend not to produce this yellow color. But the thing that you should understand is, the combinations of these things, could also produce a yellow color. So you might have an alkaline catalyzed reaction in the presence of UV light that in the presence of other catalysts might even produce a yellow color. We simply chose the simplest explanation, based on the kinds of experiments we did, and the kinds of things we saw—that the most simple explanation of what we were seeing, was that it was an acid catalyzed oxidation. That was most consistent with the facts, and required the least presumptions to justify what we were seeing. Further experiments might show that there was in fact a more complicated kind of chemistry involved. But we didn't have any test evidence for that.

<u>Case</u>: What is ionizing radiation as versus non-ionizing radiation?

<u>Dr. Adler</u>: Ionizing radiation is radiation that has sufficient energy to break chemical bonds into charged products. Non-ionizing radiation will excite a molecule so it will carry out chemistry, but it won't break the bond between the atoms in the molecule to produce charges. What ionizing radiation means is, it produces ions. So the bond breaks and leaves one part of the bond positive and the other part of the bond negative.

Dr. Heller: Ionizing radiation—ultraviolet can produce that, and x-ray of course, and radioactive radiation.

Case: And these all produce non-yellow reaction products?

Dr. Adler: Well, they don't usually lead to a yellow color.

Case: X-rays don't.

Dr. Adler: No.

Case: Not ever?

Dr. Adler: Well, not, not ever, because if you had other kinds of chemicals in a long series of reactions, then again it might lead to a yellow color. That's why we're worried about what kinds of contaminants are there. For example in the municipal Turin air, you have acidic air pollutants. You realize the problem there? If the image is what we say it is, then over a long period of time, the background cloth color is going to come to the same color as the image is, and the image will disappear.

Dr. Heller: The image will be lost.

Dr. Adler: Which means people better start getting worried about conservation of the cloth.

Case: Oh, that's what you were getting at in the article you wrote in *Shroud Spectrum International* [#42, December 1993, ed. Dorothy Crispino.]

Dr. Adler: That's the point of the conservation article.

Case: And just rolling it up and keeping it in that box won't do the trick.

Dr. Adler: It won't do the trick.

Dr. Heller: No.

Case: Well, in my opinion it's lasted for 2000 years, and so . . .

Dr. Heller: Have you ever gone to your grandmother's house, for Easter or something like that? And see the old linen table cloth brought out, and seen how it had gotten brown and brittle?

Case: Yes.

Dr. Heller: That's oxidation. From the atmosphere.

Case: How does heat turn linen yellow?

Dr. Adler: Well, heat can also cause a faster rate of oxidation, just like catalysts. You're delivering energy to something, in terms of molecular motion, or infrared radiation, which gets absorbed by molecules and causes them to heat up. It's just an evidence that the molecules are excited. If I put a fire under your chair you'll soon feel the heat, because the molecules in your pants and your rear end would feel excited.

Case: How does it burn or scorch, then?

Dr. Adler: Because if you get it hot enough, if you put enough heat into it, the bonds break. Then you get chemistry.

Dr. Heller: In my book, I went through the arguments that Dr. Ray Rogers used. He's a thermal chemist. And he said, given the temperature of the shroud in the fire, that's a beautiful thermal experiment. And we know it was hot enough to melt silver. So he had one theory to discount, temperature-wise, i.e., a painting. If it was an organic pigment, the temperature would have turned the color into some other color.

Dr. Adler: We can actually get down to your question, which is kind of interesting. Why does heat turn linen yellow? Because it's an oxidation reaction. What exactly is heat? It is just temperature producing, excited motions in chemical structures. How does heat produce a burn or scorch? Because it increases the rate at which these reactions take place. Can heat produce an acid type oxidation\dehydration? Of course it can. Now the thing that's interesting is though, because it's hotter, it will produce reactions beyond what we think is the thing that made the image. You can actually see in the fluorescence pictures—you can tell the difference between the scorch and the image, under fluorescence conditions. If you heat it hot enough, some of the reactions begin to break down the sugar structure of the cellulose, and you get a compound called furfurals. And these furfurals fluoresce orange under ultraviolet excitation. And we see something pretty interesting. Because when you look at an ultraviolet excited photograph of the Shroud, you actually find that the scorch images [from the fire] do fluoresce orange, because they were produced by scorching.

<u>Case</u>: But the image doesn't.

<u>Dr. Adler</u>: But you find that the image doesn't. And so that tells you immediately that the Shroud image was not simply produced by an elevated temperature. So that's why we say it wasn't. And that's why Dr. Heller said it wasn't, in the book.

You have to use different pieces of the physical and chemical evidence, all at the same time. That's how you draw scientific conclusions.

<u>Case</u>: So it couldn't have been a high temperature kind of thing.

<u>Dr. Adler</u>: If it had been, the image would fluoresce orange.

<u>Case</u>: So whatever made it, had to be a low temperature . . .

<u>Dr. Adler</u>: Had to be something that was done at a comparatively low temperature. And Dr. Sam Pellicori also explored that in one of his papers, also. What temperatures would produce the degree of oxidation we see in the image? Also, that same type of chemistry can be found in the cellulose literature—you know there's a lot of independent literature that bears on the same kind of chemistry as the Shroud.

<u>Case</u>: The contrasting shades producing the Image demonstrate a pattern similar to halftone prints (like photos in newspapers). That is, a particular darker area is not made up of darker fibrils, but of a higher percentage of colored fibrils . . .

<u>Dr. Heller</u>: Right.

<u>Case</u>: . . . than is the case in lighter areas. No single fibril is darker than another in the image—within a certain small range. Is there any heat, light, or other radiating source that could conceivably produce such a selectively localized oxidation effect?

<u>Dr. Heller</u>: No. Mind you, you're talking about a forgery.

<u>Case</u>: Well, no. I'm talking about conceivably in any way. Say, any natural by-product of something supernatural, for example.

<u>Dr. Adler</u>: Well, we haven't found an explanation. It's one of the interesting things about the Shroud. It's an areal density,

not a concentration density. Variations in shade are produced by the number of fibers that are discolored and not by the amount of "pigment" that's applied. And, one of the mysteries of the Shroud is that no one has an explanation of this. Not even John Heller.

Case: Not even you [Dr. Heller]?

Dr. Heller: No.

Case: Is it fair to say that the image is "scorch-like" but has characteristics that make it impossible for it to have been produced by any known natural process?

Dr. Heller: It's got the same color as a scorch, a light scorch. That's the only way it's "scorch-like." It does not fluoresce orange.

Dr. Adler: Let's go back a bit. Is it impossible for it to have been made by any known process? We made "Shroud image" fibers from modern linen. So you can't say there's no natural known process. We simply took linen, soaked it in sulfuric acid, which is a dehydrating, strong oxidant, and made "Shroud" fibers. With exactly the same chemistry. Does that mean somebody painted the image with sulfuric acid? Well, it would chemically produce what's there, but then you've got to explain how you get all the physics that's there. It's an optical problem—the 3-D effect. There are plenty of chemical processes that will produce the chemistry of the Shroud. There are plenty of physical processes that will produce the physics of the Shroud. What you have to do is find one that will produce the physics and the chemistry at the same time.

<u>Case</u>: Right.

<u>Dr. Adler</u>: And if that's not bad enough, you have to also require that it produce the biological characteristics of the Shroud at the same time. And it's interesting that no matter what anyone has suggested, they haven't found a mechanism that will correctly explain the biological, physical and chemical characteristics all at the same time.

<u>Dr. Heller</u>: You can't forget that science is very probabilistic.

<u>Case</u>: Dr. Eric Jumper and Dr. John Jackson (members of the 1978 STURP team that investigated the Shroud in Turin) derived a 3-D image of the Shroud on a VP-8 Analyzer, which is a sophisticated instrument usually used for analyzing photos taken in space. Dr. Jackson says the 3-D image produced by the analyzer requires that the "rays" from the body would have had to go in a straight line from the body to the Shroud at each point, impinging perpendicularly to the plane of the Shroud. No light or heat source could manage this—they would produce a scatter effect. (Except a laser—you brought that out in your book). Right here, do we not have to infer a purposeful supernatural cause, rather

than a quasi-natural bi-product of the body suddenly radi-
ating or flash-heating?

Dr. Adler: The answer is, we don't know. Just because we
don't know, doesn't prove it's supernatural. It just means,
we don't know a process that can do this. Well, a lot of people have tried some of these things, physically, and people
have tried to find theoretical explanations. John Jackson has
come up with a couple. But not all of us buy what he thinks
are some of the mechanisms. Because they seem to violate
other physical laws.

Case: Let's get to the 1988 C14 dating. The samples sent to
the three testing labs (in Arizona, Zurich and Oxford) all
came from the same area on the Shroud. The three samples
are actually three parts of one sample. Does the theory of
C14 decay indicate that all areas of a plant or animal will
start out with the same amount of C14?—So that the C14
"clock" will always start at zero no matter where a tiny sample is taken?

Dr. Adler: That's a pretty tricky question. For several reasons. One, if you look at an isotopic variation of a molecule.
Suppose you look at carbon dioxide with C12 in it versus
C14. The C12 isotopic molecular structure will react faster
than the C14 one will, so if you carry out a series of chemical reactions, you're going to find that the ratio of C14 to
C12 varies, depending on the particular chemical structure
you look at. So if you radio-date a whole plant, the C14 date

you will get from the plant as a whole, will be different from the C14 date you will get from the cellulose in the plant; different from the protein you get from the plant. Because it will have undergone a different amount of what people call biofractionation. Which a chemist calls a kinetic isotope effect. This is the point that has been brought out by these two Russian scientists, Kouznetsov and Ivanov, who tried to explain some problems with the C14 date. However, that's not the problem with the sample. The samples of cellulose all taken from the same amount, the same kinds of plants at the same time in the same area, would all be expected to show more or less the same C14 date.

Dr. Heller: Right.

Dr. Adler: But the real problem in the radiodate sampling, is, a sample of the C14 taken from the middle of the cloth will not necessarily give the same C14 date as the area they took the sample from—on the side of the cloth.

Case: Because there's a variation in the C12/C14 ratio . . .

Dr. Adler: Because you only took one sample. So you can talk all you want about how reproducible the date is, but you can't talk about how accurate it is. You have no way of knowing if the area you took the C14 sample from represents the whole cloth. That's an area which has obviously been repaired. There's cloth missing there. It's been rewoven on the edge. They even cut part of it off, because it was obviously rewoven on the edge. The simplest explanation why the date may be off is that it's rewoven cloth there. And that's not been tested.

Case: You can verify that, that it's rewoven right in that area?

Dr. Adler: You could, but it hasn't been tested.

Case: You said it was rewoven.

Dr. Adler: You can see that the edge of it has been rewoven. Which they cut off.

Case: And how far do those threads go into the sample?— I see.

Dr. Adler: It also is near the burn mark. And it's water-stained. So you don't know if chemistry has taken place to make it different from the rest of the cloth. And in fact this Russian explanation of why the date's off would depend on it being near enough to the fire to produce this kind of change. They've actually done an elaborate set of experiments where they've demonstrated that a fire could change the date. They don't know whether that applies to the Shroud or not.

Dr. Heller: That's interesting work, incidentally.

Case: The actual spread of uncalibrated dates from the three labs extended from 1090 A.D. to 1390 A.D. The early date comes from "O1.Lu" at Oxford, and the most recent from "A1.1B" at Arizona. And even these extreme dates are averages of a number of different "runs." Is this spread enough to make the dates "iffy"?

Dr. Adler: Yes, but not 1000 years "iffy."

Case: OK.

Dr. Adler: Part of the problem with the uncalibrated dates, is that they haven't been what they call dendrochronologically corrected [by dates ascertained by counting tree rings]. And so you find out that the spread is less, for the corrected dates.

Case: Right. But still, the original measurements are way, way different from each other. However, the three labs all had pretty close hits on the three control samples of known age. Would you agree that the problem with the dates lies not in the methodology of the C14 tests, but in some unrecognized contamination in the Shroud sample itself?

Dr. Adler: It could be that or it could be a sampling error, because they only took one sample.

Dr. Heller: But no, there's no methodological problem with the carbon 14 testing as it was. I don't doubt that.

<u>Case</u>: Habermas and Stevenson, in *The Shroud and the Controversy,* (which, incidentally, is the only book I've seen that's been written since the C14 testing) mention a secret C14 test of the Shroud that supposedly took place at the University of California nuclear accelerator facility in 1982. Two ends of a single thread were assayed at 200 A.D. and 1000 A.D. respectively. Do you have any knowledge of this "secret" test? The only source the authors give is "News release, 14 October 1988."

<u>Dr. Heller</u>: I do.

<u>Case</u>: You do? Could you verify that something like that happened?

<u>Dr. Heller</u>: Yes.

<u>Case</u>: How do you know?

<u>Dr. Heller</u>: I sent the sample to the guy who tested it.

<u>Case</u>: Where did you get the sample?

<u>Dr. Heller</u>: I got it from the Shroud.

<u>Case</u>: You got it from the Shroud and sent it to the University of California?

<u>Dr. Heller</u>: Yes.

<u>Case</u>: And they tested that thread.

<u>Dr. Heller</u>: Yes. But again, that was only one test.

<u>Dr. Adler</u>: And again, it's in the same dubious area of the Shroud. It's from the same area as the "Raes" sample taken in 1973. The same area as the 1988 test.

<u>Case</u>: Well, two ends of a single thread, that give 800-year-apart dates, and then another sample from the same general area with other dates, means the whole thing is fouled up.

<u>Dr. Adler</u>: That's because one end of it was starched.

<u>Dr. Heller</u>: We found a lot of starch in the fiber.

<u>Case</u>: Would starch give a more recent date or a more ancient date?

<u>Dr. Adler</u>: It depends on when the starch was put on. You should know that the test was not performed under rigorous conditions; the dates were not corrected by the dendrochronological curve; we do not even know which end—the starched end or the other end—gave the earlier date; the experimenter was not experienced in C14 testing. The results of that 1982 test should be thrown out.

You see there are a lot of problems in taking your sample for C14 testing. The amazing thing is, the archaeologist who advised on the protocol for doing the [official 1988] test, Bill Meacham . . .

Case: I know. There was a seven-lab protocol . . .

Dr. Adler: Well, before that meeting. I was at that meeting too, as the chemical advisor. It was written up in *Archaeological Chemistry IV.* Bill pointed out all the things that you could screw up if you didn't have an archaeologist involved in the sampling, to advise you what to do and what not to do. And a chemist, to tell you what to do and what not to do, before you start sampling. That was all in the original protocol. *They didn't follow it.* They wrote a different protocol. *They didn't even follow that.* When asked why they took the sample where they took it, the answer was: "Well, it was cut there before." Now that is the stupidest argument in the world for taking one sample from the place where they took it. Because they know that area is an area that's been repaired; they know it's by a water stain; they know it's by a scorch; and they know that people have found previous chemical evidence that that area is peculiar. But nevertheless, that's what they did. And that's why we have a date that all sorts of people don't believe. Because they don't believe the accuracy of the thing.

Dr. Heller: You know the guy that took the sample? He's not a trained scientist. He hasn't even got a Bachelor's degree in science.

<u>Case</u>: The people who took the sample obviously didn't have any realization that the carbon 14 test would be completely screwed up by these various inadequacies in getting the sample.

<u>Dr. Adler</u>: You can't say they hadn't been warned those things would happen. They decided willfully to ignore them. Do you want to know what the answer was?

<u>Case</u>: Yes.

<u>Dr. Adler</u>: They were sure the date was going to come out right. That's what I think. They were so sure the date was going to come out right, that they ignored all the things people told them about that, to put it in plain English, would screw it up. And so we are all paying for the fact that they were so sure it was going to come out right, they could ignore everybody's advice.

<u>Case</u>: Can linen exposed to air over many centuries pick up atmospheric carbon, thus adding C14 to the sample over time, resulting in a too recent date?

<u>Dr. Adler</u>: One of the interesting things that these Russians have done is to have offered evidence that that in fact can take place. They haven't published this yet, but it's going to come as a shock to a lot of people who have been doing cloth testing. In fact they're suggesting that this can be a way you can test cloth better than doing C14 testing. Because you

detect some of these small molecular changes.

Case: What is "carbon exchange" and under what conditions does it occur? Under pressure cooker conditions, for example steam from water in the 1532 fire?

Dr. Adler: Well, the interesting thing about this Russian fire model is: to the extent that you burn cloth under oxidizing conditions, the cloth ordinarily tests older instead of younger. The thing that these Russians did that was unique is, they didn't burn it in open air. They reacted linen in an atmosphere of combustion products. Carbon dioxide, carbon monoxide, water molecules at controlled temperatures. The same thing that might have happened during the fire.

Case: So they reproduced the Shroud fire . . .

Dr. Adler: They reproduced conditions occurring in the fire. To everybody's amazement, the dating went in the opposite direction. The cloth tested younger instead of older. Now, we still don't know if that really is true for the Shroud. We only know it's true for a cloth that's been put under the conditions of the Shroud fire.

Dr. Heller: Again, it's probabilistic.

Case: OK. This question is along the same lines. Your book states that you found carbon from the fire. Could some of this carbon have come from a non-Shroud source, such as the backing material, or through holes burnt into the silver box, and ultimately from surrounding tapestries or burning walls? Do you have any speculation about that?

Dr. Heller: Anything is possible. But if the carbon monoxide and carbon dioxide which was produced, exchanged with the carbon of the sample, as in the Russian model, you would expect that you would get a more recent date.

Dr. Adler: By the way, it couldn't have come from the backing cloth, because it didn't have a backing cloth at that time. The backing cloth was put on to strengthen it after the fire.

Case: Oh. OK. Would you explain the "khaki" effect that produced the iron oxide particles in the water stain margins, particles that were found *inside* the closed tubular fibers? Would such chemical reactions taking place under extreme conditions produced by the fire have any relevance to a possible accelerated carbon exchange in the fibers themselves?

Dr. Adler: We discovered that in the 1800s some of the people living in India produced khaki by staining with iron salts, putting it in alkali, and then letting it dry out, to make iron oxide, producing a khaki color. So, we decided to try the same experiment, and we discovered, hey, what do you know, it puts particles inside the fibers. That's because they get in there in solution and precipitate, under those conditions. They form iron oxide on the inside. They don't have to come in from the outside. They are formed on the inside.

That can happen, as we pointed out in the paper, during the fire. The stuff would have gotten on the inside, and over a period of time it would have precipitated and then dried out at the time of the fire. So in fact the fire would have relevance to this kind of "khaki" evidence. And it could also have produced carbon exchange. That's the whole point of the Russian paper.

<u>Case</u>: Given the massive contamination by human touching, smoke, contact with various fabrics, etc., over the centuries, could carbon from this surface contamination be forced into the chemical make-up of the cellulose fibers during the extreme heat and steam produced by the fire?

<u>Dr. Adler</u>: Not very likely. It would take a lot of it. Much more than you'd expect from the conditions of the fire itself.

<u>Case</u>: You both co-authored an article setting forth the results of chemical testing of the Shroud which appears in *Archaeological Chemistry – III*. Here I quote: "There are areas on the body-only image that are relatively lower in optical density than other areas in relation to the background. Most noticeably these areas appear as stripes running longitudinally on the Shroud and are due to the different lots of thread used in the manufacture of the cloth." And later on: ". . . Inhomogeneous lots of thread resulted in the apparent effect of stripes appearing to run laterally and longitudinally the length of the cloth. The stripes are undoubtedly due to the fact that different lots of thread will show different

degrees of degradation. We know that the body-only image is due to advanced degradation of the cellulose. Hence, it is perfectly consistent that the body-only image also reflects these same differentials."

Isn't this to say that the Image didn't "take" on these striped areas?—Simply due to a slight difference in the cloth?

Dr. Adler: You have to be careful here. It doesn't mean the image didn't "take." It just means these different lots of thread may have started out at different acidities, and so the reaction "went" to different extents. We're talking about an acid catalyzed oxidation. There's already acid there, in the structure of these batches of fibers. So my explanation is simply that this lot of fiber was more oxidized to begin with, therefore more acidic, and so you get a darker image than in the other lots of fibers.

Case: How many of them are there? The stripes?

Dr. Adler: Nobody's ever counted them, because nobody's really interested in that kind of a problem. Unless it affects the interpretation of the image.

Case: These aren't the same things that are called restorative patches?

Dr. Adler: No. These are something very different. These are stripes that go the whole length and width of the cloth.

So you see it's a batch of threads employed in the weaving of the cloth itself. While the patches are obviously patches. You can see them. They were added.

<u>Case</u>: And the stripes can't be accounted for by folding of the Shroud rather than "different lots" in manufacture? And that therefore something radical in its chemical effect took place after the original image was formed and while the Shroud was folded?

<u>Dr. Adler</u>: The stripes couldn't be accounted for by folds in the Shroud. The Shroud would have to be folded over 100 times in random and strange patterns. John Jackson's done a lot of work on that.

<u>Case</u>: In other words, the stripes we are talking about don't conform to the folding pattern at all.

<u>Dr. Adler</u>: Right.

<u>Case</u>: You've already answered my next question, about the sample being taken from near a repair area.

<u>Dr. Adler</u>: They were taken from a stupid area, to put it in plain English. And you're right, they were from a water-stained area, and near a scorched area from the fire. The Russian paper claims that that is good reason for doubting the date.

<u>Case</u>: I figured that in 5700 years, half the C14 would decay; after 2000 years, 18%; and after 700 years, 6%. This means that about a 12% increase in the C14 counted would give a date 1300 years too recent. Comment?

<u>Dr. Adler</u>: Wrong. The problem is, the decay is not linear. It's exponential. That's the physics of it. And what you mean by these percentages—all sorts of people have screwed this thing up. There's a better way of saying it. To have the date be over one thousand years off, you'd have to replace 40% of the carbons by modern carbon—to get the right ratio (of C12 to C14) to make it turn out right. That doesn't mean you'd have to replace it by C14. It means you have to take C14 in a ratio to C12 that's here now today. But you would have to replace 40% of the carbons. Now if you had some crazy mechanism that would selectively replace C14 atoms, then it would take a much smaller percentage. And what these Russians seem to have found is a mechanism that will in fact do that. Because they're talking about what is known as a kinetic isotope effect, and that's very clever.

<u>Case</u>: I see from a table in *Radiocarbon: Calibration and Prehistory,* that a 10% contamination of a 1000 year old sample by new carbon would result in a C14 date that would assay at only 160 years old.

<u>Dr. Adler</u>: You have to be careful to know what they mean by that. That's just what I'm driving at. Is it something that is added to the sample? Is this something that's replaced in

the sample? Are they talking about putting in 10% C14, or 10% carbon with a ratio of C14 to C12 that is presently in the air? One of the troubles with these things is that people make all these kinds of comments. You take something that's 1000 years old. That means it's already decayed along this exponential curve. And now what he says he's going to do is, he's going to take it at this present date and he's going to add modern carbon to it with its ratio.

Case: Right.

Dr. Adler: So that starts decaying from now. The combination of these two produces a different clock time. But it's not a linear clock. It's an exponential clock. 10% modern carbon with its ratio of C14 to C12, added to a 1000 year old sample with C14 to C12 with its ratio, decaying till the time the new carbon was added, would look like a carbon 14 to carbon 12 ratio that reads at 160 years. And he's probably correct. But you can't then turn around and say, Well, if we think the Shroud was 100 A.D., and we dated it at 1350 A.D.—you can't extrapolate these numbers that you've got, because you're calibrating linearly. You can't extrapolate linearly. You have to go through the exponential calculations. That's why there's all kinds of literature where people have made all kinds of ridiculous remarks because they don't understand the fact that this is in fact an exponential calculation. It's the physics of the way radioactive materials decay.

Case: So you are saying again that . . .

<u>Dr. Adler</u>: Let's say you start with a sample that's got a radioactivity of one. And it's got a half life of say, a year. That means in one year it drops to one half of what it had. In two years it drops to one quarter of what it had. It drops by a half again. In three years it drops to one eighth of what it had. Half again. It isn't just dropping in a linear way. It's dropping in an exponential way. That's a lot harder to think about. You have to calculate it. Not just sit down with a piece of paper and a ruler and draw lines—which a lot of people have done for this. You also have to watch out, because you are not at liberty to pick any old year you want to talk about that you want to put into the experiment. Because you have this problem of the $C14$ to $C12$ ratio. In any given instant in time it isn't constant. If you are going to do this honestly you have to make this dendrochronological correction.

<u>Case</u>: I know. You have to plug in this calibration curve I saw [in "Radiocarbon Dating of the Shroud of Turin," *Nature,* vol. 337, 16 February 1989].

<u>Dr. Adler</u>: And some of those variations are very big. By ignoring that, you can come up with all kinds of crazy things that are off by a couple of thousand years.

<u>Case</u>: Say that in the fire, a whole lot of carbon got exchanged, or came in.

<u>Dr. Adler</u>: It could change the date back to the date we see. That's the point of the Russian's argument.

Case: And you are saying that a 40% change would do that.

Dr. Adler: Well, no. Because that would be if you didn't have any kinetic isotope effect.

Case: Which is what?

Dr. Adler: This is this thing I told you about where the molecules don't react at the same rate. And so you can have more C14 added to the structure than C12.

Case: Oh. It keeps getting more complicated.

Dr. Adler: You see there's no way you can simply calculate this. You actually have to sit down with the right physics and do the physical calculations, starting with the right dates, when you think things happened, with the right corrections. It's a very complicated calculation.

Case: But this was done in that paper you were talking about, that the Russians wrote.

Dr. Adler: This is the Kouznetsov-Ivanov paper. And they claim because people ignored all this, that the same thing happened to the Shroud, corresponding to the results they found in the laboratory experiments, the Shroud can easily be 2000 years old. They can't prove it's 2000 years old but they can prove that if these kinds of conditions obtained, it could easily be that.

<u>Case</u>: Assuming for the sake of argument that the Resurrection took place, could the "radiation" from that event involve neutron bombardment of the Shroud? I see that in a letter in *Nature,* Feb. 16, 1989—the same issue in which the laboratory reports were presented—Thomas J. Phillips of Harvard University presents a similar notion: that neutron bombardment of a certain amount would change enough C13 (another isotope of carbon) to C14 in the Shroud to produce a date 1300 years too recent. Do you have any comment?

<u>Dr. Adler</u>: Yes. I met Tom Phillips. We talked about this. He actually is an IBM scholar. He works for IBM, but he works in some of these other laboratories. He's a theoretician. And he's right. And he actually suggested a way it can be tested. He pointed out that if that's what happened, you look at a ratio of chlorine isotopes. The fact is, nobody has looked. Nobody's had enough sample to look. It's an experiment that calls for a fairly large piece of sample. So here's a theoretical explanation that would work, but it hasn't been tested.

John Jackson, by the way, has suggested a number of other radiation type things that would do this. He pointed out that if you had borates as a water contaminant, on the Shroud, from dousing the fire, there's a series of nuclear reactions that would lead to excess C14. I actually tested that for him. I ran tests for borates. They're not there.

<u>Dr. Heller</u>: Unless you can reproduce the Resurrection, the entire neutron theory goes down the tubes.

Case: This is entirely speculative. I realize that. We have no idea what the Resurrection would have produced, naturally—as a natural effect. OK, what about these mildew spoors you found? But no mildew?

Dr. Adler: People have seen things that correspond to fungi, pollens, all kinds of things, including bacteria. In fact, one of the things we suggested they better find out is, is there biological degradation? It's never been tested. And it's a serious problem in the conservation. But one of the reasons you wouldn't find mildew is because it hasn't been kept under damp conditions. So even if it were there, you wouldn't expect a lot of it there. I think the comment John [Heller] made was that many other cloths from this time and area have been mildewed to death. Because they weren't kept under the same conditions as the Shroud was.

Case: I thought that STURP as a whole found just mildew spoors, but that Dr. Frei, who took those samples in Turin . . .

Dr. Adler: STURP never did any biological testing. Riggi, the guy who took the C14 sample, at the time of the STURP testing, collected dust from the back of the cloth, and analyzed it for spoors, and pollens, and whatever else he could find. He found mites, and he found certain kinds of bacteria, and he cultured it, and he found fungal spoors. I don't know if they are the kind that would make mildew or not. But there is certainly fungi on the Shroud. And one of the points we've made for conservation is you'd better find out what types and how much, because if you don't, you're not going to be able to conserve it properly.

Case: Then you don't want to make any comment on this: that if there is no apparent biological degradation—actually we don't know how much—

Dr. Adler: We have no idea. This is something that would have to be determined.

Dr. Heller: There's bound to be biological degradation. Biological cells are omnipresent in the environment. And a lot of them love to eat carbohydrates and polysaccharides.

Dr. Adler: In fact it's one of the points we've raised about the conservation. You'd better not talk about conserving it physically and chemically until you find out what's there. One of the things you'd like to do to conserve it, is put it under anaerobic conditions, so there's no longer any oxygen there, to oxidize the image physically or chemically. But you don't dare do that till you find out whether there are anaerobic organisms there, who would now love to multiply and divide, and live on cellulose, since there's no oxygen there to keep them at a low level.

Case: Damned if you do and damned if you don't.

Dr. Adler: Well, that's the problem with conservation. You can't do it unless you find out what's there.

<u>Case</u>: You noticed that there is little apparent aging of the Shroud, though it exhibits a degree of yellowing from age. It is quite supple and retains lateral and diagonal strength and flexibility . . .

<u>Dr. Heller</u>: Right.

<u>Case</u>: Do you have a comment about that, or is it just another mystery? You would expect it to be much more brittle . . .

<u>Dr. Heller</u>: I don't know the answer.

<u>Case</u>: I've been leading up to another conclusion, or another speculation anyway. Since there was no discernible biological degradation of the Shroud over time, and little apparent chemical degradation, and these in themselves denote something unnatural; what if there were also no, or slowed, radioactive decay?

<u>Dr. Adler</u>: You can't really conclude that. The fact of the matter is, the conditions under which it's been kept for most of it's known historical history, in the dark, in a closed box, under a reasonably maintained dry condition—it hasn't really had much of a chance to do any of these things. So until somebody produces another piece of cloth which has been kept the same way, you can't say whether this is unnatural.

<u>Case</u>: Yeah.

<u>Dr. Adler</u>: Nobody's ever done the experiment.

<u>Dr. Heller</u>: There are mummy cloths, which is the closest thing that we have. There is a lot of that around.

<u>Case</u>: And most of that from ancient times is quite caky and, as soon as you touch it, it flakes.

<u>Dr. Heller</u>: Right.

<u>Dr. Adler</u> [to Dr. Heller]: Didn't you see some cloth from Diuropus [an archaeological site in the Near East] which is even earlier and which is in good shape?

<u>Dr. Heller</u>: Yes.

<u>Dr. Adler</u>: That's only because its been kept under similar conditions as the Shroud. That was what? 3000 B.C.?

<u>Dr. Heller</u>: Right.

<u>Case</u>: What chemical and physical evidence is there indicating an age of the Shroud much older than the putative age as determined by C14 testing?

<u>Dr. Adler</u>: None other than common sense. They only took one sample from one place. You can't say anything about the accuracy. Now, there have been tests suggested that could be run on samples that would unequivocally determine that the

accuracy is wrong. They haven't been run. Because there aren't sufficient samples to do them.

<u>Case</u>: Well, what other evidence of age—would you say the forensic evidence say, of a crucifixion . . .

<u>Dr. Adler</u>: No. But there's plenty of evidence that says it's not a painting. That doesn't prove it's the right age. In fact there's something you'd better understand from the start. All the science in the world is never, ever going to prove the Shroud is authentic.

<u>Dr. Heller</u>: Right.

<u>Dr. Adler</u>: It's only capable of proving it's disauthentic.

<u>Dr. Heller</u>: Even if you had a signature on the lower right hand side, "This is my Shroud, signed J. Christ. Attested to by the mayor of Jerusalem." That's not scientific evidence. That's historical evidence.

<u>Dr. Adler</u>: To make a scientific conclusion you have to perform an experiment. There is no acceptable laboratory experiment for "Christness." We pointed that out to people four or five times in print, and nobody pays any attention. It's not true to say that scientists are trying to authenticate the Shroud. If you want to be honest you have to say that scientists are testing to see if the Shroud is disauthentic. Because a single scientific test could disauthenticate the Shroud.

Case: Hmmmmm . . .

Dr. Adler: Such as the radiocarbon date. But that means you've got to be sure that there's nothing wrong with the radiocarbon date.

Case: Ummmmm . . .

Dr. Adler: Science can only confirm the consistency of an historic argument that this cloth belongs to this particular man. There's no scientific test ever that's going to tell us the identity of the man whose image is on the Shroud.

Dr. Heller: On a probabilistic basis again, that man had even more things done to him than was said in the New Testament, in the Four Gospels, and he died a suffocation death, which is what you do when you are crucified.

Case: All those kinds of indications indicate that what we have is a real crucifixion.

Dr. Heller: Yes.

Case: And crucifixions didn't take place after something like . . . about 300 A.D.?

Dr. Adler: 333 A.D. was when Constantine ruled them out, but interestingly enough you find historic examples, that people seem to do it here and there through time. Barbara

Tuchman in her *Distant Mirror* describes crucifixions taking place in much later Medieval times, during some of the various religious persecutions. But it wasn't widespread after Constantine.

<u>Case</u>: Giles F. Carter, a chemist at Eastern Michigan University, theorizes (in a paper also published in *Archaeological Chemistry – III*) that long wavelength x-rays from elements on the surface of the skin formed the image. He says that attenuation of these x-rays in air over different distances from the Shroud could produce a fairly undistorted 3-D image. Do you have any comment on the hypothesis?

<u>Dr. Adler</u>: Giles's stuff is pretty interesting. But he didn't get the right chemistry for the blood, though it did account for the image. Also he didn't give some of the right biology. There are some people backing that as an explanation though.

<u>Case</u>: To finish up: what I want to say is that empirical science cannot prove authenticity, but if you rule out everything that you can possibly conceive of, the whole electromagnetic spectrum, a scorch produced by heat, anything natural . . .

<u>Dr. Heller</u>: I think we ruled out that it was made by the hand of man.

<u>Case</u>: Therefore, it was made by something other than the hand of man.

<u>Dr. Heller</u>: yes.

****

That was it. I was overjoyed. I thought, "Wow, have I got a great interview!" I drove home that evening thinking "at last, we have a marriage of science and religion!"

In retrospect I wonder about the curious reserve exhibited by even these two honest scientists. "Science" can't prove the Image is that of Jesus Christ? Not experimentally, of course. But if you eliminate all natural possibilities, are you not faced with the logical necessity of a cause beyond nature? And if you add the forensic evidence (the scourge marks conforming in imprint to the First Century Roman *flagrum,* the wound in the side, bleeding from the crown of the head)—evidence which conforms in every respect to the Gospel accounts of the Crucifixion—then are you not forced to conclude that this is indeed the burial shroud of Christ? It is not a matter of going beyond science into faith, but rather—in this case—confirming a miracle by means of science.

A comment made by Dr. Adler near the end of the interview must be corrected. He says that "a single scientific test could disauthenticate the Shroud. Such as the radiocarbon date. But that means you've got to be sure there's nothing wrong with the radiocarbon date." The fact is, even if the radiocarbon date as it stands were correct (and there are good reasons to think that it is *not* correct), the conclusion would be that the Shroud came into existence around 1300 A.D., but it wouldn't tell us *how* it came into existence. With a negative scientific conclusion as to paint or human artistry of any kind, with a positive scientific conclusion as to oxidation of the fibers themeselves, with the optical mystery that leads us beyond physical laws—all told, what we have is either a medieval miracle or a Resurrection miracle.

It turns out that Barbara Culliton's strange little phrase in America's most prestigious scientific journal, *Science,* in July 1978, was indeed prophetic. In all these exhaustive scientific tests on the Holy Shroud of Turin, what has been attained is a spotlight, even if a little hazy in definition, on "the physics of a miracle."

END NOTE

Several times in the writing of this book, and during the interview, the hairs on the back of my neck stood up. It is of the utmost necessity to dig into the science—even if some of that science is difficult to follow—in order to refute the slew of debunking Shroud books crowding the bookstores. Only the most exacting experimental science can make the case. But once the case is made, think about this: think that this bile-ridden bright red blood so thoroughly analyzed under microscopes, doused with reagents, scorched with x-rays, manhandled and manipulated and cooked with chemicals, is the Blood of Christ.

SELECT BIBLIOGRAPHY

"A Chemical Investigation of the Shroud of Turin," J.H. Heller and A.D. Adler, *Canadian Society of Forensic Science Journal* 14,3 (1981) pp. 81-103

"An Inter-Laboratory Comparison of Radiocarbon Measurements in Tree Rings," *Nature* 298, 12 Aug. 1982, pp. 619-623

"The Mystery of the Shroud of Turin Challenges 20th Century Science," Barbara J. Culliton, *Science* 201, 21 July 1978, pp. 235-239

"Radiocarbon Dating of the Shroud of Turin," P.E. Damon et.al., *Nature* 337, 16 Feb. 1989, pp. 611-615

Report on the Shroud of Turin, John H. Heller (Boston: Houghton Mifflin, 1983)

The Shroud, John Walsh (NY:Random House, 1963)

Copies of this book may be ordered from:

White Horse Press
6723 Betts Ave.
Cincinnati, OH 45239

For $10.50 each, plus $2.00 S&H first copy,
$.50 each additional copy

Residents of Ohio add $.63 sales tax for each copy.

Bookstores: Standard trade discount
Call 1-800-617-4551 or Fax 513-522-9675